# THE
# A TO Z
# TOUR OF TEXAS
# CITIES AND PLACES

Written by

## LINDA LEWIS MICHAEL

Illustrated by

## PATRICK LEWIS

Hendrick-Long Publishing Co.

Dallas, Texas

This book is dedicated to our parents,
Mr. and Mrs. R. E. Lewis, with whom
we shared many a tour of Texas.
Thanks for your help and encouragement.

————————————

We regret that we could not include every
city in Texas, but it is a big state.
Please accept our apologies if your city
or town was excluded.

Michael, Linda Lewis.
    *Big as Texas : the A to Z tour of Texas cities and places* / written by Linda Lewis Michael ;
illustrated by Patrick Lewis. p.     cm.
    Summary: Describes twenty-six cities and places in Texas, one for each letter of the alphabet,
from Austin and Brownsville to Ysleta and Zavalla.
    ISBN 0-937460-34-6 (pbk.) :
    1. Names, Geographical—Texas—Juvenile literature. 2. Cities and towns—Texas—Juvenile
literature. 3. Texas—Juvenile literature. [1. Texas. 2. Alphabet.] I. Lewis, Patrick, ill. II. Title.
F386.3.M53 1988
917.64—dc19
[E]                                                                                         87-36793
                                                                                              CIP
                                                                                               AC


Designed by Janet Long

ISBN 0-937460-34-6

© 1988 Copyright by Linda Michael and Patrick M. Lewis
Published by Hendrick-Long Publishing Co. Dallas, TX 75225

Is so.

Is not.

Oh, yeah?

Yeah!

I'll bet you that Texas is <u>so</u> big that there's a city and place in Texas for every letter of the alphabet, Becky Sue!

Okay, prove it, Billy Joe!

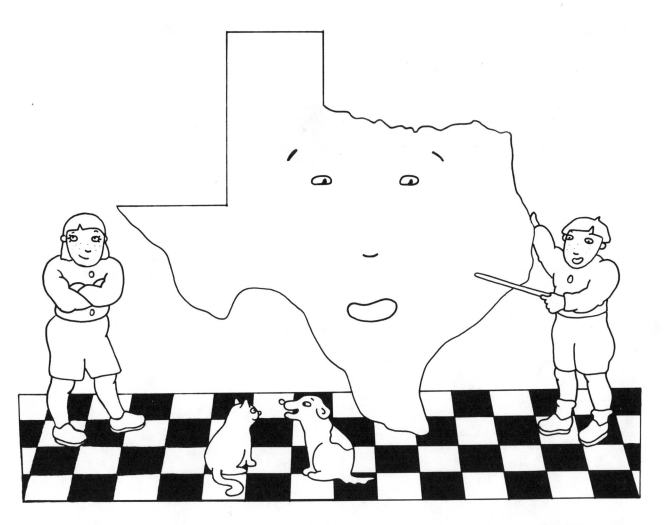

Guess what city I have in mind for the letter **A.**

I don't know. Amarillo? Alta Loma? Abilene?

No, Becky Sue. You're not even close.

How am I supposed to guess without a little hint, Billy Joe?

This city is the home of the Lyndon B. Johnson Presidential Library.

Aransas Pass? Arp?

There are many beautiful lakes in this hilly city.

I know! I know! Is it right in the middle of the state?

I think she's got it!

It's our capital city Austin!

Right!

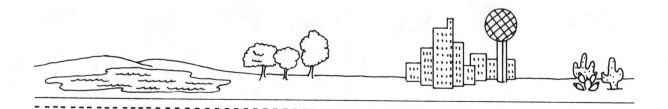

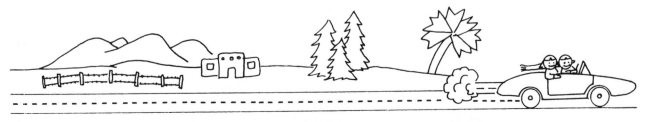

Okay, Becky Sue. That was an easy one. The city for the letter **B** used to be an important fort, but today it is a city of big business.

Fort Worth doesn't start with **B.**

Becky Sue! Think! This city's Gladys Porter Zoo protects many animals that have almost become extinct.

Borger? Big Bend? Bigfoot? Beaumont?

Wrong direction. This city is on the Texas-Mexico border. It is as far south as you can go in Texas.

Do you mean that Brownsville used to be called Fort Brown?

That's right. And for your prize, let's share a juicy red grapefruit grown near Brownsville.

Hey! You didn't guess the right answer. Why do I have to share my prize with you?

I gave you those excellent clues, didn't I? Besides, I already ate my Texas orange and I'm hungry.

Okay, but I get to give the clues for the next one, Billy Joe.

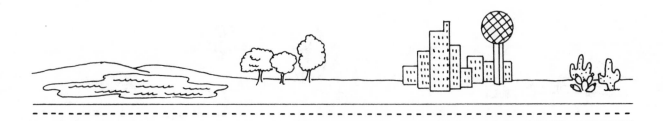

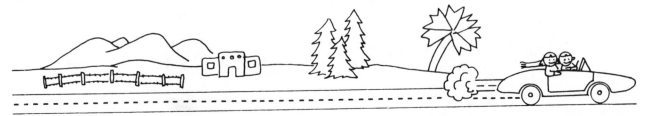

Hey, Billy Joe. I know a city that starts with a **C.**

Is it the home of the Aggies and Texas A & M University?

No, Billy Joe. It's not College Station.

How about the Spinach Capital of the World, Crystal City?

No, Billy Joe. If you'll just listen, I'll give you some clues.

Okay. Okay.

This Gulf Coast city sparkles in the warm Texas sun. Many ships dock here. There is a U.S. Naval Air Station.

Wait a minute. Let me guess. Is it named after the King of the Wild Frontier, Davy Crockett?

No, it's not Crockett, but its name does mean *the body of Christ* in Spanish.

Well, it's not Comanche.

Padre Island, the longest island in our country, is near this city. Along its beaches you might find seashells, Indian arrowheads, or maybe even pirate treasure.

Hey, hey, hey! Let's go!

You don't even know where you're going, Billy Joe.

Sure I do. I'm going to Corpus Christi!

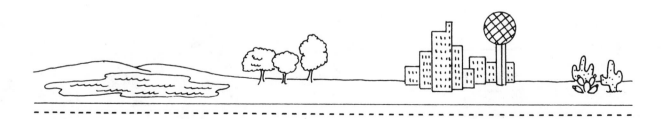

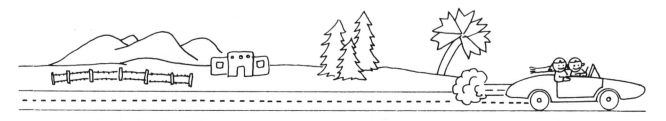

My city for **D** has the nickname of *Big D*.

Is it the second largest city in Texas, Billy Joe?

Yes! How'd you know?

Is it the home of the State Fair of Texas, the Cotton Bowl, and the Dallas Cowboys?

Who told you, Becky Sue?

Is it a fast growing city that has become an important center for banking, fashion and film making?

Okay, okay! What's the real name for *Big D?*

Why, Billy Joe, I don't have the faintest idea!

You've got to be kidding!

Sure I am, Billy Joe. *Big D* is Dallas!

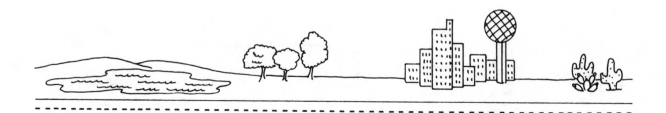

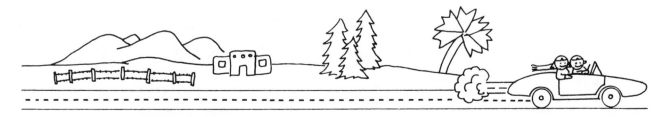

Next we're going to the city that is as far west as we can go and still be in Texas. It is the largest city on the United States-Mexico border. It began as a way to get through the mountains, so its name in Spanish means *The Pass*. Fort Bliss is a famous army base there.

Well, Billy Joe. You certainly narrowed down my choices for the **E** city. I know it can't be Eagle Pass even though it is on the border and has *Pass* in its name. Elkhart isn't on the border. Neither is Ennis or Egypt or Earth.

And I thought this was an easy one.

It is. It is. I'm just thinking, Billy Joe.

Well, hurry up. We still have twenty-one more letters to go!

All right, already! You gave it away when you told me what its name meant in Spanish. It has to be El Paso!

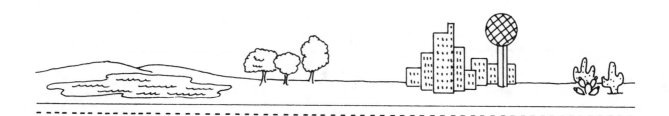

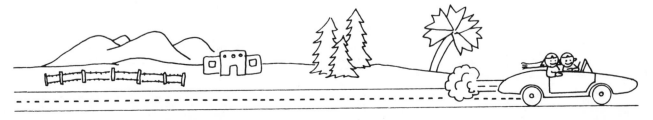

This next one is not so easy, Kiddo.

   Sure. Sure. I've heard that one before.

Well, here it is. This is an old city started by people from Germany.

   That cuts out all the cities with Spanish names.

This next part is great! There is an Enchanted Rock near this town. Indian legends tell of weird groanings and creakings coming from the ground near the rock at night.

   Wow! Are you sure we're not back at the Gladys Porter Zoo in Brownsville?

No, Silly. We're in central Texas, and the name of this city is Fredericksburg.

   Oh, that's where the Nimitz Hotel is! It looks like a ship is sitting on its roof! Inside it is the Fleet Admiral Chester W. Nimitz Memorial Naval Museum. Admiral Nimitz was born in Fredericksburg, you know.

I know. I know. Fredericksburg sounds like a good place to be born.

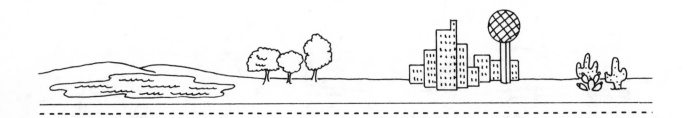

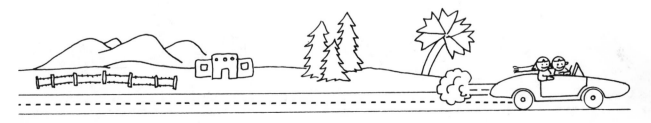

You'll love my city for the letter **G,** Billy Joe!

What's so great about it?

Imagine warm sunlight sparkling on a golden beach or wiggling your toes in toasty, tickly sand.

Tell me more!

The smell of suntan oil, hot dogs, and salty water.

Let's eat! Salt water always makes me hungry.

Listen to the waves pounding the wet sand, the noisy call of the sea gulls, and the laughter of kids splashing in the surf.

This city has a beach. Right?

Not just a beach. This city is on an island in the Gulf of Mexico. It is an international port and has an important medical school.

Does this city have a colorful history filled with Indians, pirates, submarines, hurricanes, and beautiful old houses?

You've got it!

Galveston, oh, Galveston!

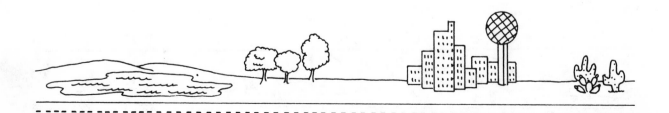

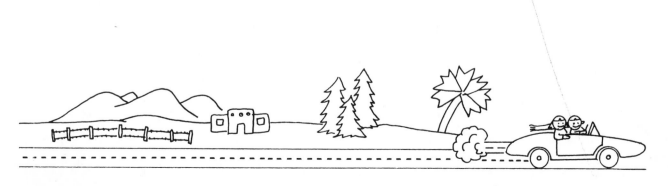

Becky Sue, go ahead and think of the next one.

Hey! This whole thing was your idea. You're supposed to think up the places.

Yeah, I know. But you did that last one so well. I could almost taste the sand in my hot dog!

Since you put it that way, my city is the largest city in Texas.

This city starts with **H,** not *Big D*. Right?

Right, Billy Joe.
It is the fourth largest city in the whole United States, Billy Joe. It is famous for so many things it almost has its own **ABC**'s.

No, that's another story.

I know. But it's famous for Astroworld, the Astrodome, and even astronauts because the Johnson Space Center is nearby.

I see what you mean.

And that's just some of the **A**'s. It has a medical center where people from all over the world come for care. This city is an important port. There are a lot of oil companies there. It . . .

Okay. Okay. It could be nowhere else but Houston!

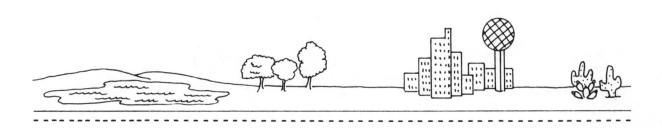

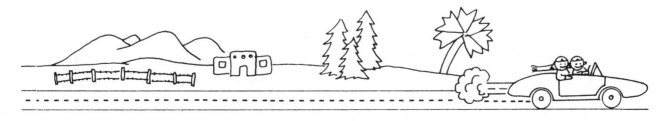

You'll never guess this one, Becky Sue.

I don't know too many places that begin with **I.**

There are bunches! I know of Idalou, Industry, Inez, Independence, Itasca, Indian Gap, and even Italy and Ireland, Texas.

Don't get wise.

Those are all cities of today. My city is an important part of the history of Texas. The French explorer La Salle is thought to have landed here in 1685.
This city was a bustling, growing port on the Gulf of Mexico in 1875. Its people planned for it to be the most important city in all of Texas. Then a hurricane smashed the town. It was rebuilt only to be destroyed by another hurricane eleven years later. For some reason, these Texans decided to move to a safer place. Today, only a statue of La Salle looks down on the waves and broken buildings.

How sad. You're right. I'll never guess.

This city of forgotten dreams is Indianola.

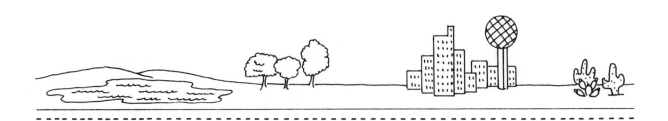

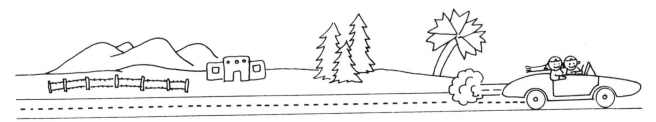

So much for past dreams. How about a city that kind of stands for a man's hope for the future?

> I'm ready, Billy Joe.

This city is in the hill country. It was named for the relatives of a famous man.

> There are lots of cities in the hill country named for relatives—Brady, Castroville, Elroy, George West, Geronimo, Mendoza, Roosevelt, Sisterdale, Twin Sisters . . .

Hold it. None of those relatives start with **J**.

> Oh, I forgot.

So just listen, already!
Visitors to this city's Pedernales State Park enjoy waterfalls, swimming, birds, and animals. There is a special park where the 36th President of the United States grew up.

> But what about the dream for the future?

I'm getting to that.
This man cared a lot about poor people. He tried to make things better for them so they could have a brighter future.

> Let's see . . . 36th President. Hmmm . . . Lyndon B. Johnson was from Texas.

Remember the Lyndon B. Johnson Presidential Library in Austin? Mr. Johnson's ancestors started Johnson City.

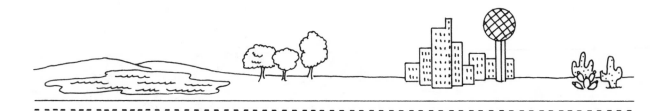

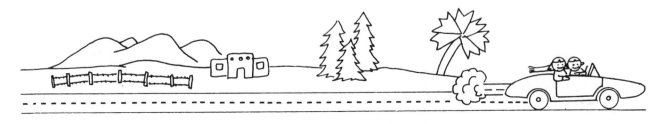

Home, Home on the Range!

I guess the mystery **K** city has something to do with ranching, Billy Joe.

You're right as rain, Pardner.
Our **K** city is the home of Texas A and I University.

Doesn't sound like a cow to me.

The cows—all kinds of them—are a little south of there. They are on the largest ranch in forty-eight states. These ranchers even developed their own kind of cattle— the Santa Gertrudis breed.

Okay, Smarty. Are we talking about the ranch or the city?

Well, the names are almost the same. The ranch is the enormous King Ranch.

And the city?

Kingsville!

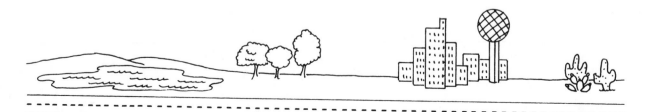

My **L** city was built to settle an argument.

I had nothing to do with it!

Silly. This was way back in 1891.
These townbuilders were fighting over where in the High Plains to build their town.

I'll bet there were lots of places they could have chosen.

Finally they agreed on the site of my **L** city. For a while, that was about all any of the early settlers agreed on. They complained about the tumbleweeds, prairie fires, and sandstorms.

I'd complain too with all that dust!

Not today. There are so many flowers there that this city is known as the Chrysanthemum Capital of the World.
It is the home of Texas Tech University and Prairie Dog Town.

This city has a little bit of everything. High Plains, huh?

I'll go easy on you and tell you. It's Lubbock.

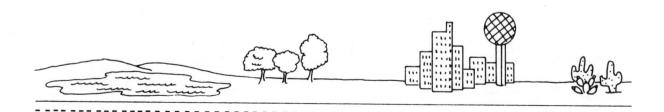

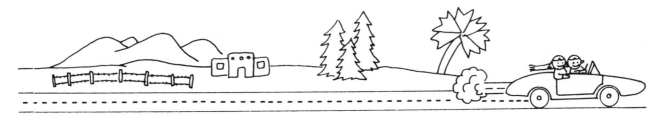

Imagine golden sunlight sparkling on sand. Wiggling your toes in warm, tickly sand . . .

> Hey, I already did that one, Billy Joe. It was Galveston. Remember—beach, medical center, submarines?

This is different. We are in West Texas.

> You've got to be kidding! A beach in West Texas?

I didn't say anything about a beach. I said, *sand*.
My **M** city is known for its pecans, its oil, and a very unusual state park. This park is like a giant sandbox with acres and acres of huge sand dunes.

> Sounds like fun, but I sure don't know what its name is. Why couldn't you have picked Muleshoe with its statue of a mule? It was built to honor all the hard work mules did for the pioneers.

Nice story, but wrong city. There were some camels in Texas at one time, though. In 1855, the U.S. Army experimented with camels as pack animals around Camp Verde in Kerr County. The ground there was a little too rocky for the camels, and the experiment was stopped when the Civil War began. The camels might have been a little more at home if the Army had taken them further west to what is now the Monahans Sandhills State Park near the city of Monahans, Texas.

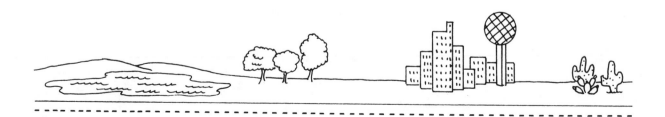

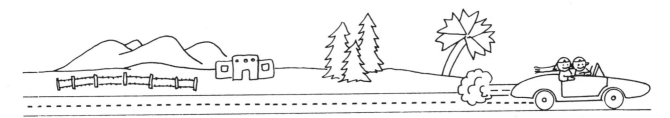

Let me do one, Billy Joe.

I'll guess it. **N** cities are easy. Let's see—North Zulch? Nocona? They make boots there, you know. Nederland was named for the Netherlands and has a big windmill. Nome? New Braunfels?

Cool it. Give me a chance. You're not even close.
This East Texas city is one of the oldest cities in Texas. It began as a trading post and fort. In fact, the Old Stone Fort is still there. It's on the campus of Stephen F. Austin State University.

Can you guess why Notrees was named Notrees?

That's way off the subject. My city was named for the Nacogdoche Indians.

What else could it be but Nacogdoches?

What else?

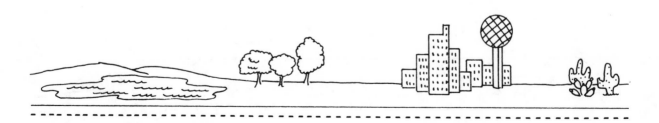

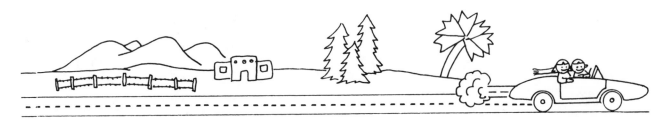

Let's go back to West Texas for our **O** city, Becky Sue.

That's a long way from Nacogdoches.

It's not as far away as some Russian railroad workers were from home when they came to work in Texas. They were homesick and named our **O** city after their hometown in Russia.

That was nice. Was their home near a sea?

We're in West Texas, remember? Not the Gulf Coast.

Well, you said there was the sand of the beach in Monahans in West Texas.

This city was built on land that was once an ancient sea. That's why, today, it is an area rich in oil and natural gas.
Nearby, there is even a gigantic hole in the ground where a meteor from space crashed into the earth over 20,000 years ago.

I'm afraid I wasn't born then. Can you tell me anything more recent?

This city has the world's largest jack rabbit.

Really? Is it the home of the Easter bunny?

The jack rabbit is a ten foot tall statue, and the city is Odessa.

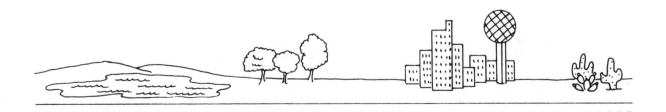

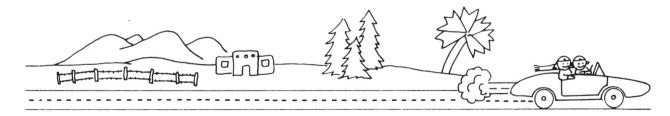

There are a lot of interesting places in Texas that start with **P,** Becky Sue.

Name one.

Paint Rock, Paris, Penelope, Pecos, Presidio, Port Aransas, Plum, Palestine . . .

I said <u>one</u>.

Presidio is one of the hottest places in the country. Paint Rock has prehistoric Indian paintings on a nearby cliff . . .

Okay, okay. I get the idea. Now give me the clues for **P.**

This is a place, not a city. It's a very big, deep place. It is in the Panhandle near Canyon and is the largest state park in Texas. The last great Indian battle in Texas took place inside its steep walls.

This is a canyon near Canyon. Right?

This canyon has many colors in its soil. There is a musical play presented outdoors in the canyon during the summer.

The name is on the tip of my tongue, Billy Joe.

Sure it is. It's Palo Duro Canyon.

Oh, I was thinking of Pasadena.

Pasadena?

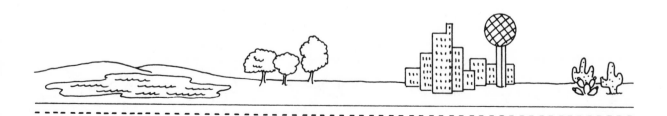

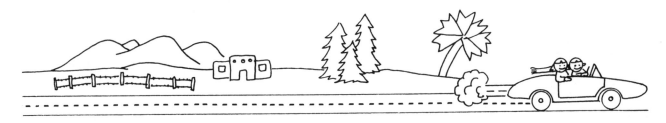

I'll bet you don't have a city for **Q**, Billy Joe.

I have six cities as a matter of fact.

Sure.

Quail, Queen City, Quitman, Quemado, and Quitaque.

That's only five.

Do you think I'd give this one away?

I was kind of hoping.

This city is named for the last great Comanche chief. His mother, Cynthia Parker, had been captured by the Indians when she was a child. When she grew up, she married the chief of the tribe. This town was named for their son.

Interesting. I'd like to know more. What's his name?

Not so fast. Outside of town are four tall hills that rise from the flat land around this North Texas town. The Indians thought these hills were magic.

Wow! I give up. Tell me.

Quanah, Texas, was named after Quanah Parker, chief of the Comanches.

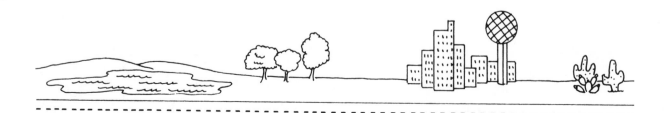

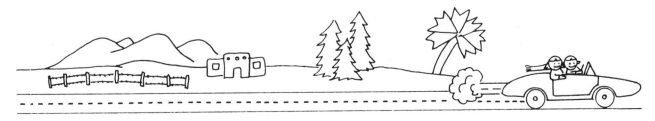

I know a city in Texas that is on the Gulf of Mexico and has a giant crab and the biggest live oak tree in all of the state.

Does the crab live in the tree, Becky Sue?

The crab is a statue honoring the crabbing industry. The tree is for real in Goose Island State Park.

I know it's not Rockwall, the tiniest county in Texas.

You can catch a boat called the *Whooping Crane* that will take you from this city to the Aransas National Wildlife Refuge. You can see many endangered species, like the whooping crane, and all sorts of animals if you are quiet and alert.

Quiet and alert. That leaves us out.

My city is important to tourists and fishermen.

Rising Star? Round Rock? Rice? Ropesville?

My city is Rockport.

Round Rock sounds almost like Rockport.

Sorry, Billy Joe. Almost doesn't count.

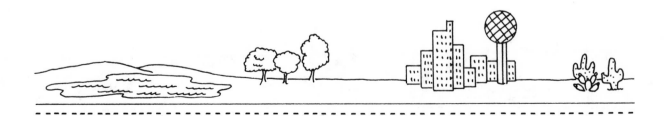

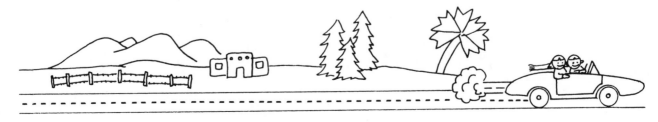

This one is easy, Becky Sue. It is the third largest city in Texas. A beautiful river winds through its parks, hotels, restaurants, and the whole downtown. There is a great zoo. There is even a tiny model circus in the Hertzburg Circus Collection. It is a very modern city with an important history. It is most famous for its missions. The mission where so many brave men died for Texas' independence is here in San Antonio. It's called the Alamo.
Oops! I gave it away!

I already knew it was San Antonio.

Oh, I could have picked Seguin, home of the world's largest pecan.

It's a statue. Right?

Right.
Then, there are the beautiful caverns of Sonora and Sugarland—named after its leading industry . . .

I get the picture. Let's go on to **T.**

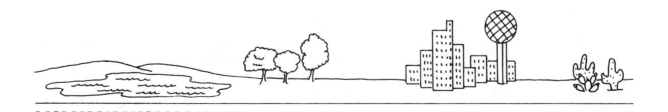

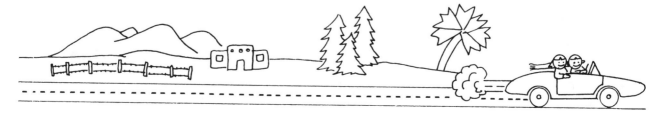

My city for **T** is famous for its flowers—especially its roses. Its roses are shipped all over the world.

> Are you sure you're not talking about Lubbock again with its chrysanthemums?

No. Roses.

A famous football player comes from this city. They call him the *T_____ Rose.*

> The *T_____ Rose?* What does that mean?

You know. The name of the city goes in the blank. I'm not giving this one away. This East Texas city was named for President John T_____.

> President John T_____, huh? John Texarkana? John Tarzan? John Terlingua? John Turkey or Telephone?

Really now.

> Those last names are all cities in Texas, Billy Joe.

How about John Tyler? How about Earl Campbell, the *Tyler Rose?*

> Well, how about that? The name of this town must be Tyler.

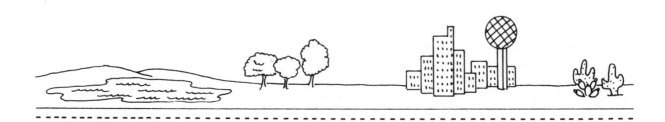

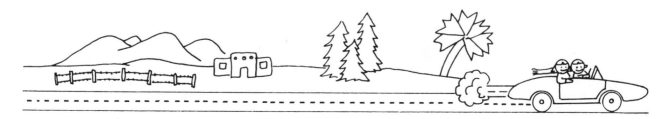

This next city can claim three famous citizens.

How come I've never heard of all your famous people, Billy Joe?

I've heard there is a difference between ignorance and stupidity, Becky Sue. Which are you?

Never mind. Go on.

A long time ago this city was the home for a frontier sheriff and outlaw named J. K. *King* Fisher.

Sheriff *and* outlaw?

Times were tough.

Near this town is Garner State Park, named for John *Cactus Jack* Garner, a Texan who was a vice-president of the United States. Vacationers love to camp there and float down the Frio River on inner tubes.

Sounds like fun.

Today this city is an important ranching and farming center and the home of a former governor of Texas, Dolph Briscoe.

Tell me and I'll take you tubing.

You've got a deal. Let's go to Uvalde!

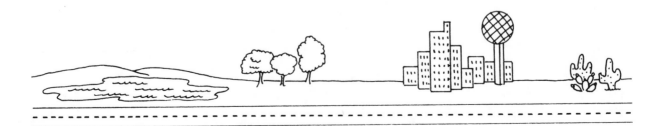

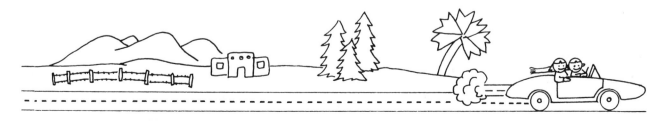

My city **V** means victory in Spanish and was named for a man who later became the first president of Mexico.

Victory, huh?

The first artificial ice in the South was made there in 1868.

Remind me to send them a thank you letter in about July.

The town was one of the first three towns to become official cities in the Republic of Texas. Its newspaper is the second oldest continuous newspaper in Texas.

What's going on there today?

It's a busy, important city. Its Texas Zoo only has animals native to Texas. They don't live in cages but in displays made to look like their real homes. Lots of people have visited this city during its International Armadillo Confab and Exposition.

The armadillo is the state mammal of Texas, you know.

I know, but you don't know the name of my city. I might as well tell you. In Spanish, *victory* is the city of Victoria.

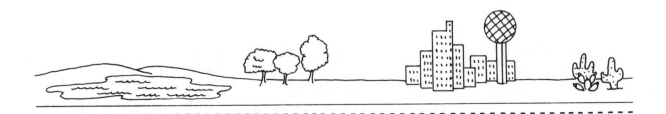

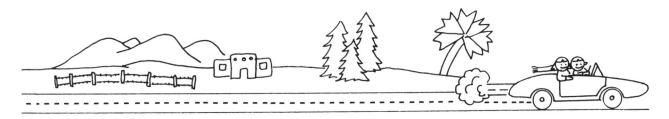

There was an Indian tribe with the same name as our next city.

Have you noticed how many places in Texas have Indian or Spanish names?

The Indians and Spanish are very important to Texas history.

And I thought it was only the cowboys.

The city for **W** was part of that wild and wooly cowboy past. Its nickname was *Six-Shooter Junction!*

Wow! I'll bet there were Texas Rangers all over the place!

As a matter of fact, today there is a museum there dedicated to the Texas Rangers.

Lots of wild things went on there, huh? How about today?

Speaking of wild, this city has the Central Texas Zoo and lots of bears.

Bears? In the zoo or on the streets?

On the streets. Baylor University is there, and their mascot is a bear. Get it?

Very funny. This city has to be Waco, named for the Waco Indians.
I guessed it! I guessed it!

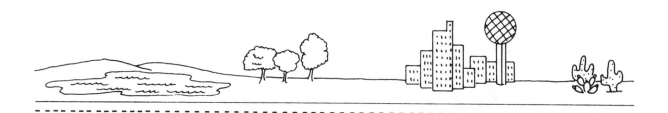

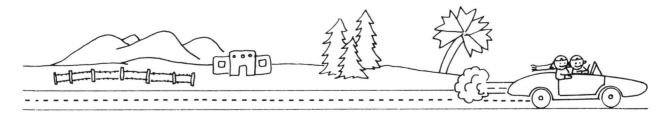

Okay, Becky Sue. If you're so smart, you come up with a city for **X.**

I was afraid of that. How about a place instead of a city—a giant place?

You mean you really have one, Becky Sue? Wow! I'm impressed. It was the one letter that really gave me trouble.

It's simple. You just have to know your Texas history.
In 1882, the Texas government had a lot of land but no money to build a capitol. A deal was made to trade land for the money. This land became known as our **X** place because it took up almost ten counties in the Panhandle.

Wow! Ten counties!

The name means *Ten in Texas*. It was the largest fenced ranch in the world.

Ten doesn't start with an *x*, Becky Sue.

Think of ten in Roman numerals, Billy Joe. Ten is *X*. The word *in* gives us *I*. *T* stands for Texas. The *XIT Ranch*—Ten in Texas.

Is there still an *XIT Ranch?*

Yes, there is, Billy Joe, but it's a little smaller now. We still have the capitol, too. Remember Austin?

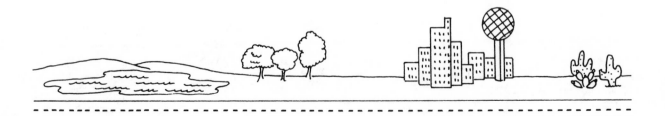

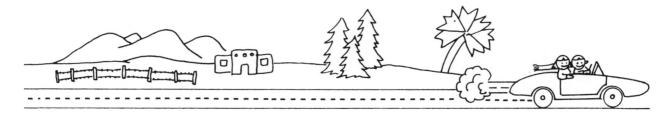

We have been all over Texas, Billy Joe. Where to next?

Let's go to the oldest town in what is now called Texas. Today it is part of the far West Texas city of El Paso. It is a city of tall buildings and small whitewashed adobe houses. Many of the houses have doors and window frames painted blue to bring good luck.

My house has a brown door.

So what?
The Tigua Indians live here and dance and share their history with visitors.

I didn't know there were still Indian reservations in Texas.

Sure. There are two of them. In East Texas, the Alabama-Coushatta Indians have a reservation.

What is the name of the city where the Tiguas live?

It is called Ysleta.

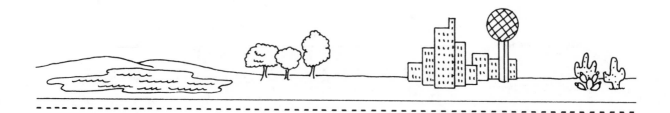

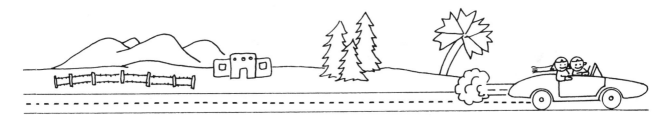

Our last city, Becky Sue! And you thought we'd never make it.

On with it, Billy Joe. You're not finished yet. **Z** is a hard letter.

You're right. But I still have a choice.
I could have picked Zella, Zapata, or Zephyr, but I didn't.

What did you pick?

This city is in deep East Texas and is surrounded by the tall trees of the Angelina National Forest. Its neighbor is a huge lake, the Sam Rayburn Reservoir. It's a great place for boating, fishing, and swimming.

How about camping? I love camping.

Zavalla is a gateway to all those fun things.

You gave it away again.

No, I didn't. I told you on purpose.

Sure you did.

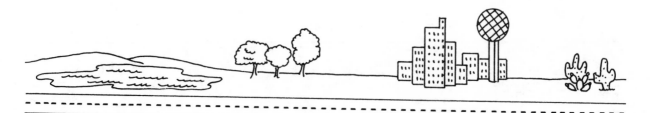

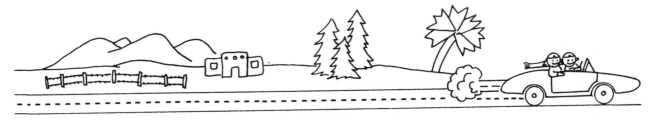

That was fun, Billy Joe. I never would have believed that there was a city and place in Texas for every letter of the alphabet!

Well, now you know. And you doubted my word!

Do you think there is an alphabet of famous Texans, or of creeks and rivers, or of plants and animals, or . . .

Whoa! Hold on! I'm not ready for this.

You need a vacation, Billy Joe.

I certainly have a choice. Which alphabet city or place should I choose?

You could pick Austin or Brownsville or . . .

Here is a way to get more information about a city. Write a letter to the Chamber of Commerce of that city. You can call the United States Post Office for the correct zip code.

Your street address
Your Town, State   Zip Code
Date

Chamber of Commerce
City, State   Zip Code

Dear Chamber of Commerce:
　　Please send me any free information you have about your city. I am ＿＿ years old. I became interested in your city by reading *Big as Texas—The A to Z Tour of Texas Cities and Places.*
　　Thank you.

Sincerely,
Your first and last names

Your first and last names                                    Stamp
Your street address
Your town, state   zip code


Chamber of Commerce
City, State   Zip Code

Ring the twenty-six alphabet cities and places of Texas. Rings may be forward or backward, horizontal, vertical, or diagonal.

```
P A L O D Y S L E T A G A U C T N
S A N T D O N Q U A N A H X O F S
I N D I A E N O L A R L O C R R P
H N Y T P V S G A L V V E T P E O
O A T Y L E R S M O N E S T U D A
M C I L A I K D A A H S N O S E N
Y O C R Y S T A L C I T Y V C R S
S G N E L C I L U B B O C K H I B
T D O A O T N L W T E N X T R C R
E O S R H D G A J A O S A O I K O
N C N F D A C S U H N S B O S S W
O H H R U O N S N S A C R C T B U
D E O E R R T S O G T D O T I U V
E S J S O I A S C I O I W H E R A
S D C A N V I L X L E E N T S G V
T E A N C X A S O H O U S T O N I
P R N A R V I K I N G S V I L L E
A I N N A L O N A I D N I V E L L
R C O T Y L C T O U V A L D E R A
O K N O S U D A L L I T L S A I I
C S Z N T B Q O S A P L E O C K R
K B A I A B U A N N A H L U B B O
P A L O D U R O C A N Y O N Y S T
O U V C L O Q M C Y H O S T E L C
R R A I T C U S T O N L I V S G I
T G L L A Y K I Z A V A L L A N V
```

| | | |
|---|---|---|
| Austin | Johnson City | San Antonio |
| Brownsville | Kingsville | Tyler |
| Corpus Christi | Lubbock | Uvalde |
| Dallas | Monahans | Victoria |
| El Paso | Nacogdoches | Waco |
| Fredericksburg | Odessa | XIT |
| Galveston | Palo Duro Canyon | Ysleta |
| Houston | Quanah | Zavalla |
| Indianola | Rockport | |

In the blanks below, match the number on the map with its correct city or place. For additional help, consult a state highway map.

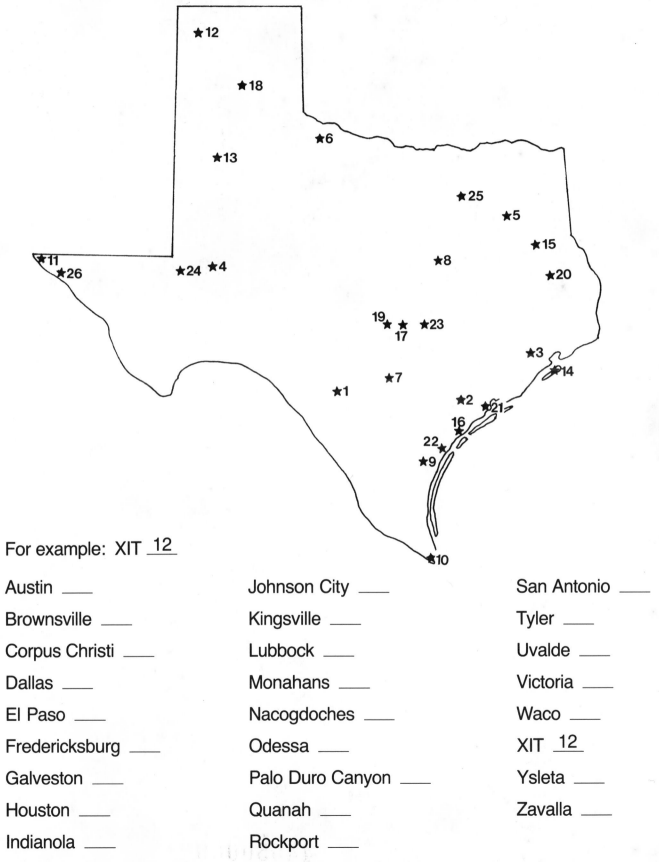

For example: XIT 12

| Austin ___ | Johnson City ___ | San Antonio ___ |
| Brownsville ___ | Kingsville ___ | Tyler ___ |
| Corpus Christi ___ | Lubbock ___ | Uvalde ___ |
| Dallas ___ | Monahans ___ | Victoria ___ |
| El Paso ___ | Nacogdoches ___ | Waco ___ |
| Fredericksburg ___ | Odessa ___ | XIT 12 |
| Galveston ___ | Palo Duro Canyon ___ | Ysleta ___ |
| Houston ___ | Quanah ___ | Zavalla ___ |
| Indianola ___ | Rockport ___ | |

# Answer Keys

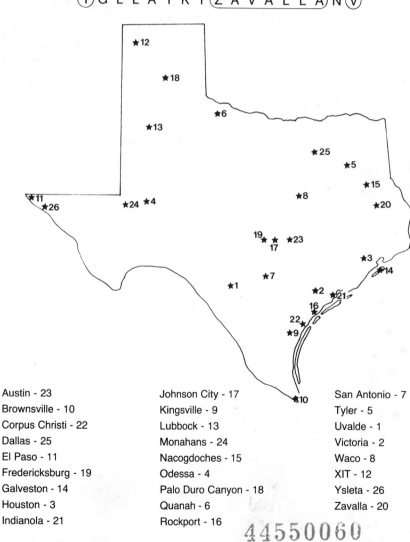

Austin - 23

Brownsville - 10

Corpus Christi - 22

Dallas - 25

El Paso - 11

Fredericksburg - 19

Galveston - 14

Houston - 3

Indianola - 21

Johnson City - 17

Kingsville - 9

Lubbock - 13

Monahans - 24

Nacogdoches - 15

Odessa - 4

Palo Duro Canyon - 18

Quanah - 6

Rockport - 16

San Antonio - 7

Tyler - 5

Uvalde - 1

Victoria - 2

Waco - 8

XIT - 12

Ysleta - 26

Zavalla - 20

**DATE DUE**

| 28 | | | |
|---|---|---|---|
| 42 | | | |
| | | | |
| | | | |
| | | | |
| | | | |
| | | | |
| | | | |
| | | | |
| | | | |
| | | | |